Clever C

Contents   **Page**

Matching color	2
Changing color	4
Seasons	6
Stripes	8
Spots	10
Two colors	12
Shape	14
Camouflage	16

written by Maria Gill

Some animals use one color to hide against the backgrounds they live in.
A snake's green or brown scales are the same color as plants.

A lion's fur is the same color as long grass. A beetle's shell is the same color as the earth. Parrots have feathers that match the leaves on the trees.

Some animals change color to match different backgrounds.
An octopus can change its color whenever it moves.

It is a light color when it is on the sand in the sea.
It changes to a darker color when it moves onto the rocks.

Some animals change color when the seasons change.
Arctic foxes change their coats twice a year.

In summer, their coats are dark, like the brown earth.
In winter, their coats are white to match the snow.

Some animals use stripe patterns to look like their backgrounds.
Zebras' wavy lines look just like wavy grass.

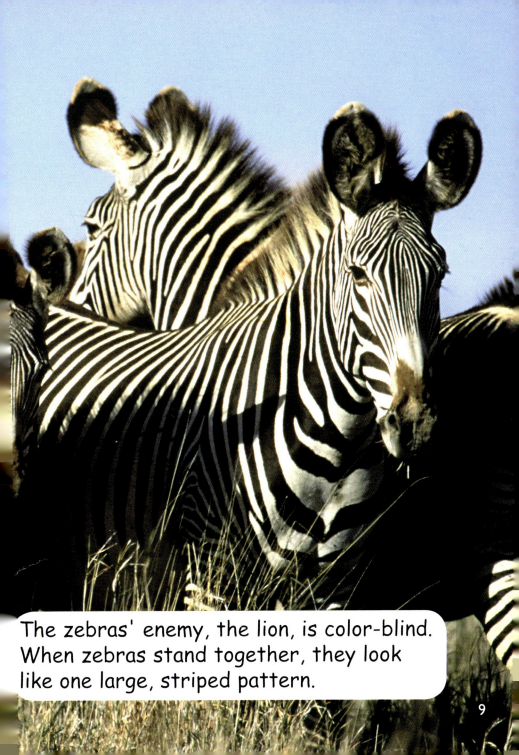

The zebras' enemy, the lion, is color-blind. When zebras stand together, they look like one large, striped pattern.

Some animals use spot patterns to hide against the backgrounds they live in. Leopards use spots to blend into the shady spots under a tree.

A butterfly fish has a large spot on the end of its tail that looks like an eye.
This makes it look bigger to trick its enemies.

Some animals use two colors to blend into their backgrounds.
The light color blends into the sunlight.
The dark color blends into the darker backgrounds.

Hungry sharks use two colors so that fish can't see them from above or from below.

Some animals use their body shapes to hide. Stick insects use their long, thin shapes to look like small sticks.

Some birds can look like branches on a tree.
A flatfish can lie flat under the sand.
A crocodile can look just like a log.

Some animals hide from the animals that they want to catch.
Some hide from their enemies that are trying to catch them.
They all use clever camouflage.